P9-APW-585

Camping Trip

An informational book

This edition first published in 2006 by
Sea-to-Sea Publications
1980 Lookout Drive
North Mankato
Minnesota 56003

Text © Deborah Chancellor 2004, 2006
Photographs © Franklin Watts 2004

Printed in China

Library of Congress Cataloging-in-Publication Data:

Chancellor, Deborah.
  Camping trip / by Deborah Chancellor.
    p. cm. — (Reading corner)
  Summary: With the help of the mother of one of them, two friends set up a tent so that
they can camp in the back yard.
   ISBN 1-59771-010-5
   [1. Tents—Fiction. 2. Camping—Fiction.] I. Title. II. Series.
PZ7.C35923Ca2005
[E]—dc22

                                                                        2004064994

9 8 7 6 5 4 3 2

Published by arrangement with the Watts Publishing Group Ltd, London

Series Editor: Jackie Hamley
Series Advisors: Linda Gambrell, Dr. Barrie Wade, Dr. Hilary Minns
Design: Peter Scoulding
Photographs: Chris Fairclough

The author and publisher would especially like to thank
Sharon and Yasmin Bowen, Kaya Allen and Rosie and
Nick Gordon for giving their help and time so generously.

Camping Trip

Written by
Deborah Chancellor

Photographed by
Chris Fairclough

SEA-TO-SEA
Mankato Collingwood London

Deborah Chancellor

"When I was little, I used to make camps in the woods with my sisters. Now, I go camping with my children!"

Chris Fairclough

"I've been taking photos for books for almost 30 years and have visited 53 countries. Every day is different!"

I packed my bag to
go camping.

I took some
food and
drink.

My friend
Kaya came
with me.

8

9

Mom helped us find a dry, flat spot.

We pushed
the poles into
the tent.

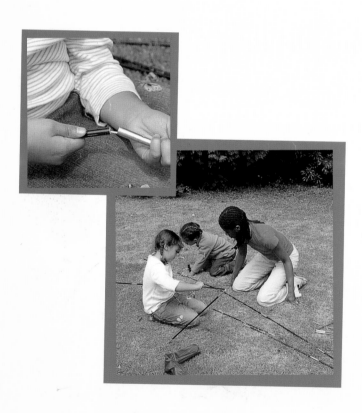

We lifted the tent up.

Then we put in the pegs.

We threw the
cover over
the top.

17

We pegged the cover down.

We pulled the ropes tight.

Then Mom
fell asleep
in the tent...

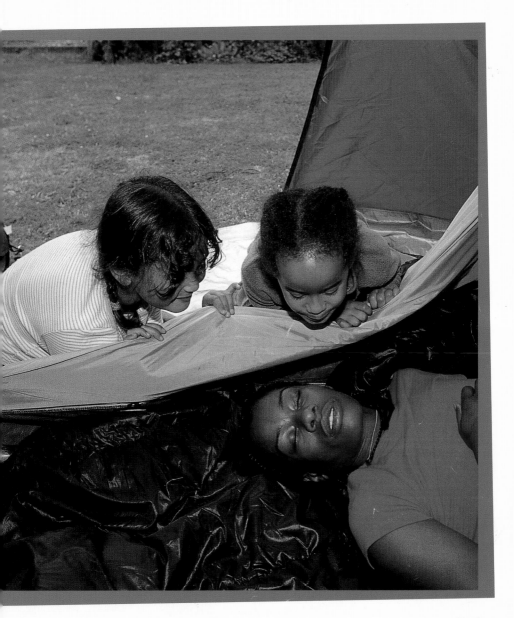

So we went
to camp in
my bedroom!

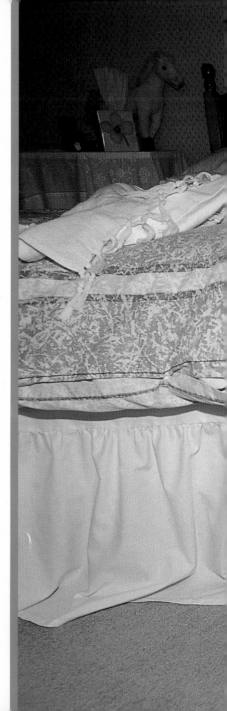

Notes for parents and teachers

READING CORNER has been structured to provide maximum support for new readers. The stories may be used by adults for sharing with young children. Primarily, however, the stories are designed for newly independent readers, whether they are reading these books in bed at night, or in the reading corner at school or in the library.

Starting to read alone can be a daunting prospect. READING CORNER helps by providing visual support and repeating words and phrases, while making reading enjoyable. These books will develop confidence in the new reader, and encourage a love of reading that will last a lifetime!

If you are reading this book with a child, here are a few tips:

1. Make reading fun! Choose a time to read when you and the child are relaxed and have time to share the story.

2. Encourage children to reread the story, and to retell the story in their own words, using the illustrations to remind them what has happened.

3. Give praise! Remember that small mistakes need not always be corrected.

READING CORNER covers three grades of early reading ability, with three levels at each grade. Each level has a certain number of words per story, indicated by the number of bars on the spine of the book, to allow you to choose the right book for a young reader:

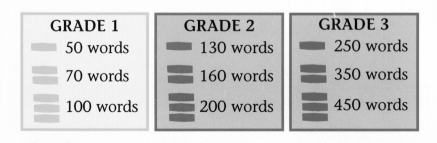

GRADE 1	GRADE 2	GRADE 3
50 words	130 words	250 words
70 words	160 words	350 words
100 words	200 words	450 words